First published in 2021 by Child's Play (International) Ltd
Ashworth Road, Bridgemead, Swindon SN5 7YD, UK

First published in USA in 2021 by Child's Play Inc
250 Minot Avenue, Auburn, Maine 04210

Distributed in Australia by Child's Play Australia Pty Ltd
Unit 10/20 Narabang Way, Belrose, Sydney, NSW 2085

Text and illustrations copyright ©2021 Gillian Hibbs
The moral right of the author/illustrator has been asserted

ISBN 978-1-78628-348-1
SJ300321CPL06213481

Printed in Shenzhen, China

1 3 5 7 9 10 8 6 4 2

A catalog record of this book
is available from the British Library

www.childs-play.com

Covered in
ADVENTURES

GILLIAN HIBBS

"Come on, Sasha," said Dad Toby.
"It's about time we got rid of that old sweater."

"Or at least let us wash it," added Dad Greg.
"Look how dirty it is!"

"Dads! It's not dirty!

IT'S COVERED IN

ADVENTURES!

The arms might be a little bit stretched by my adventures on the high seas.

The sticky patch is from our
brilliant volcano experiment.

And we all remember
where that sauce came from!"
laughed Sasha.

"I guess it is kind of wrinkled, but that's because I used it as a pillow when we went camping."

"Aha!" laughed Dad Greg. "You've certainly been busy!"

He didn't know
the half of it!

"It got really dirty when I turned it into my nature-exploring cape.

See this green patch here?
That's from when I made
the best save of the match!

And I suppose the oil was from when I was building my super-speedy go-kart.

Oh, and the brown speckles came from our muddy trail ride."

"I see," said Dad Toby. "So you're worried we might wash all the adventures away?"

Exactly! Now he was getting it!

"The blue blob is from the day we did art class outside. It was the best!

The chewed sleeve was from when that goat thought my sweater looked really tasty.

And it does have a slightly seaweedy smell...

as well as a whiff of my very
own special sandwich filling."

"Well, Sasha," said Dad Toby, "we thought you might be running out of room for new adventures."

"So we've bought you something new," continued Dad Greg. "We hope you like it!"

I loved my old sweater very much, but my dads had a point. Besides, it wasn't the sweater that made adventures happen, it was the person wearing it!

And I couldn't wait to get started on some new ones!

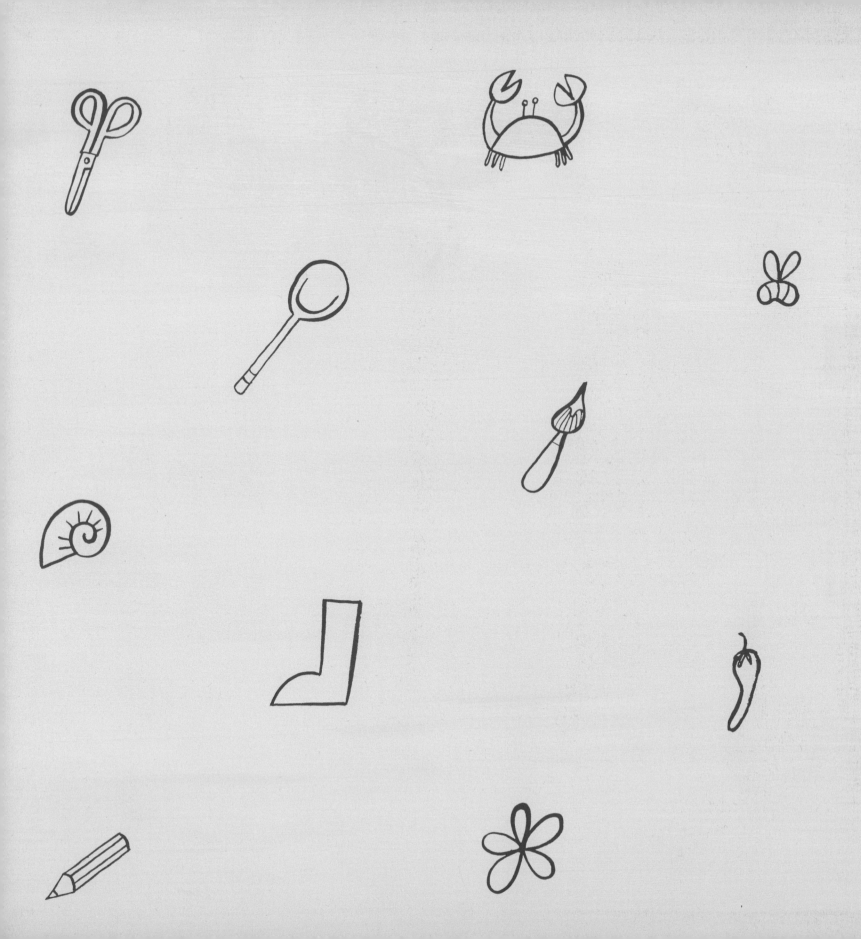